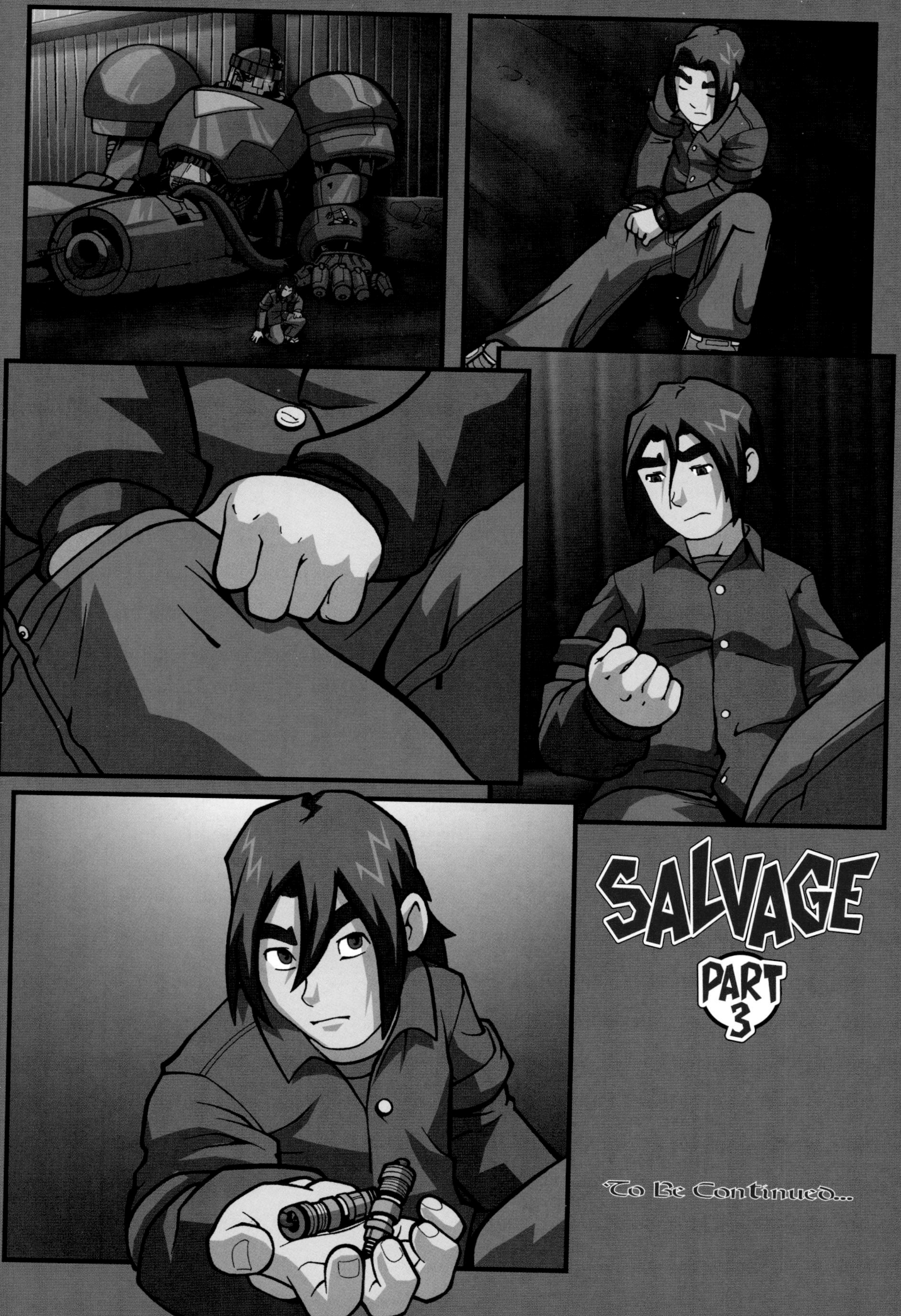
SALVAGE
PART 3
To Be Continued...

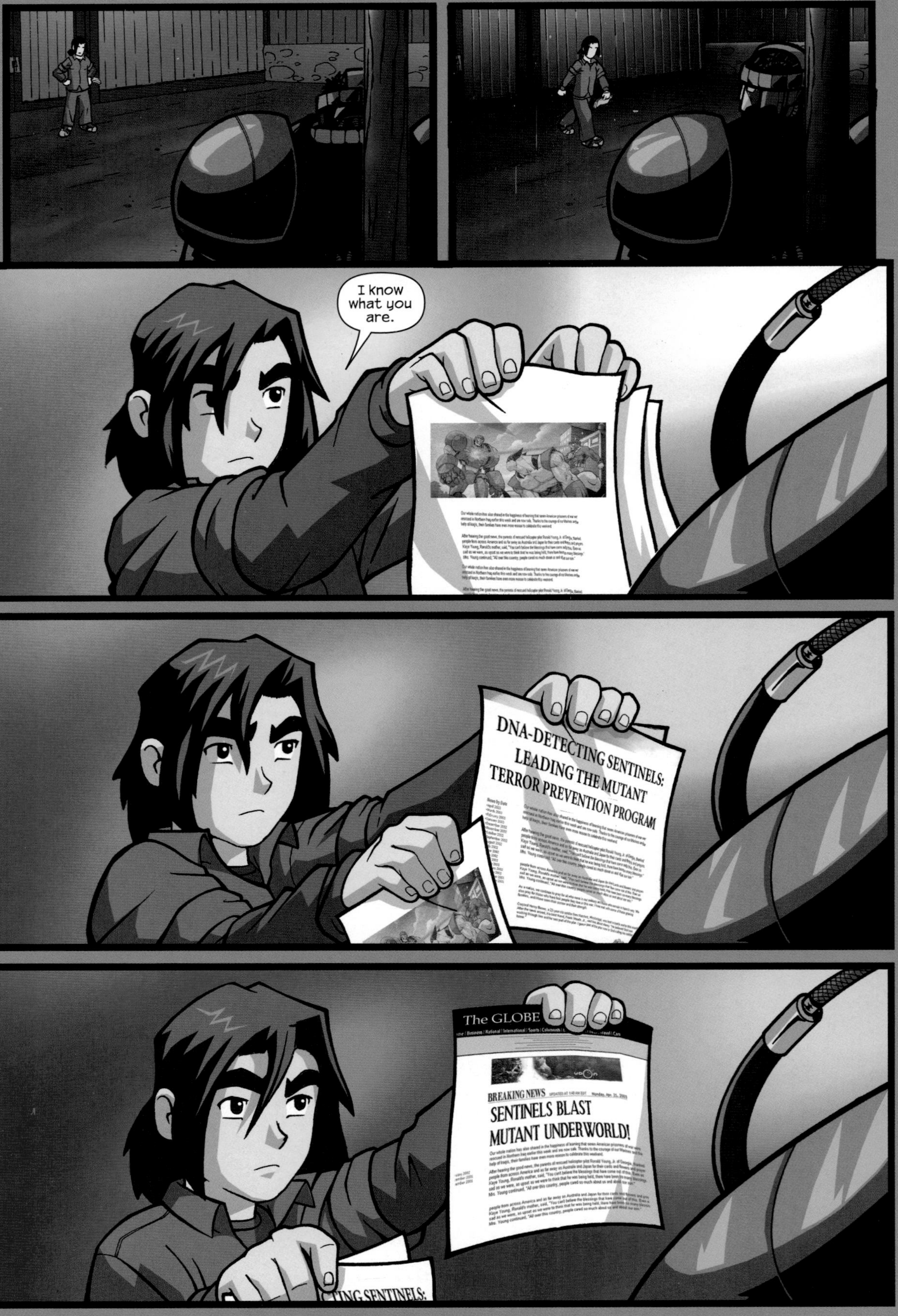
I know what you are.
DNA-DETECTING SENTINELS: LEADING THE MUTANT TERROR PREVENTION PROGRAM
The GLOBE
BREAKING NEWS
SENTINELS BLAST MUTANT UNDERWORLD!

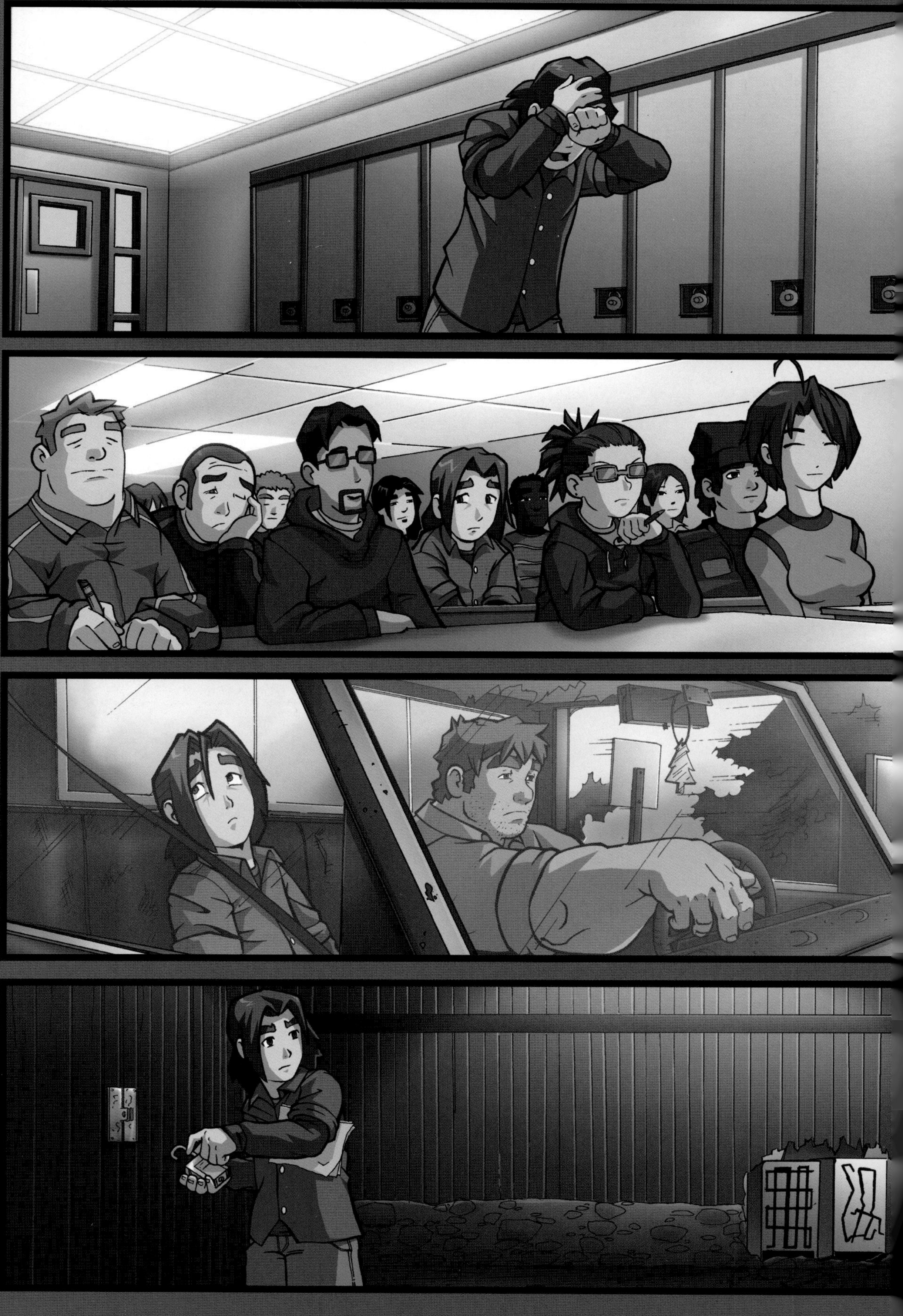

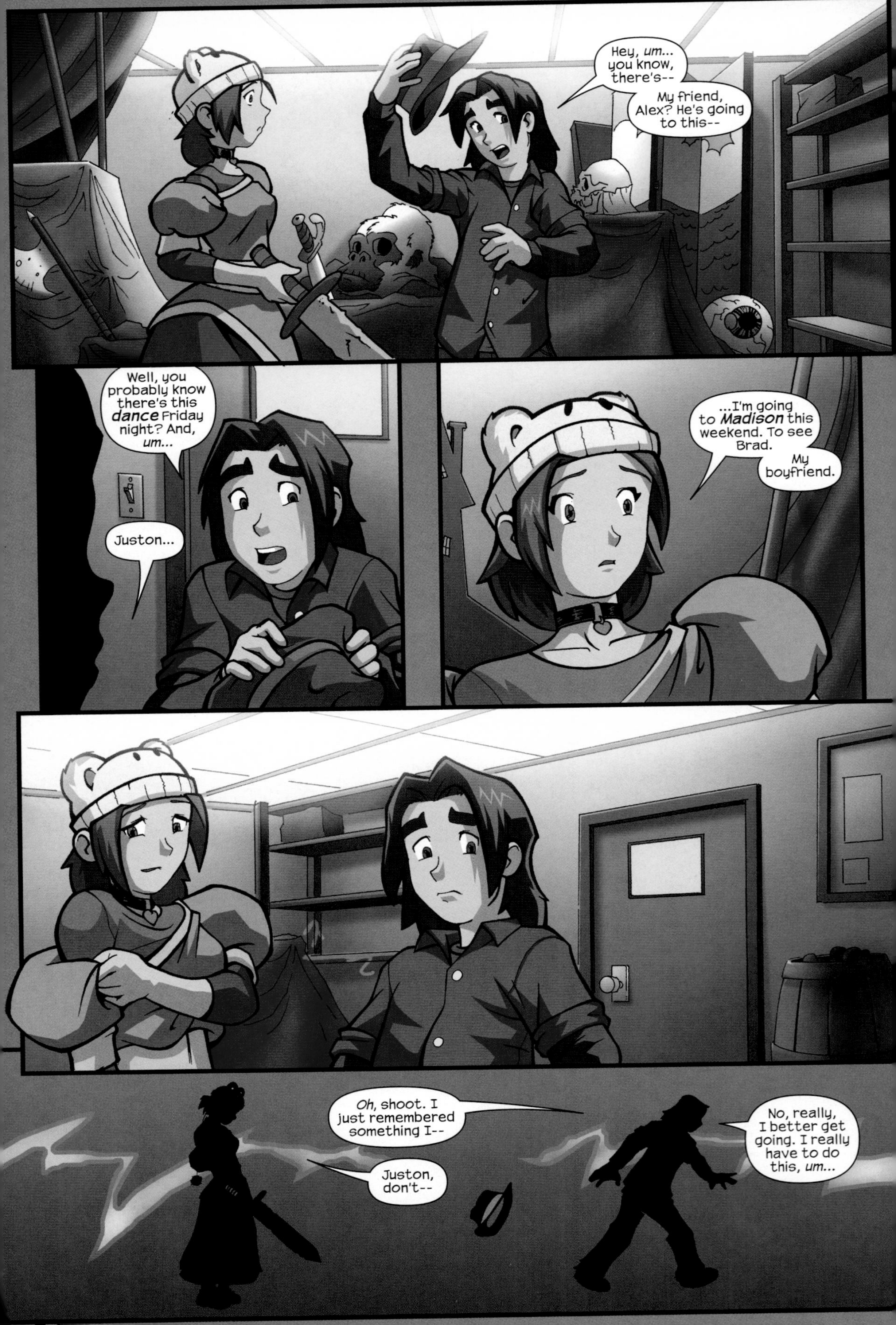
Hey, um... you know, there's--
My friend, Alex? He's going to this--
Well, you probably know there's this dance Friday night? And, um...
Juston...
...I'm going to Madison this weekend. To see Brad.
My boyfriend.
Oh, shoot. I just remembered something I--
Juston, don't--
No, really, I better get going. I really have to do this, um...

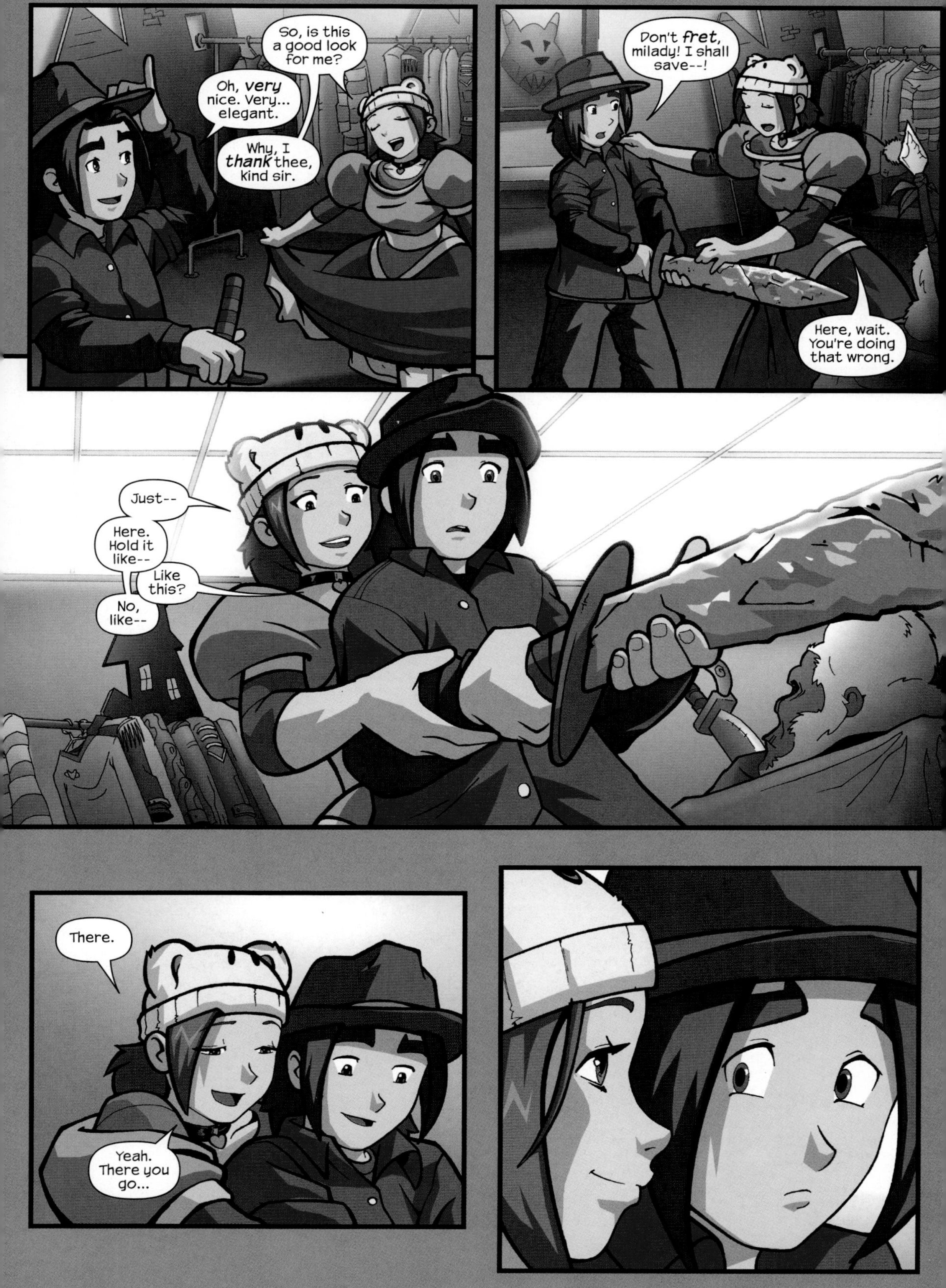
So, is this a good look for me?
Oh, very nice. Very... elegant.
Why, I thank thee, kind sir.
Don't fret, milady! I shall save--!
Here, wait. You're doing that wrong.
Just--
Here. Hold it like--
Like this?
No, like--
There.
Yeah. There you go...

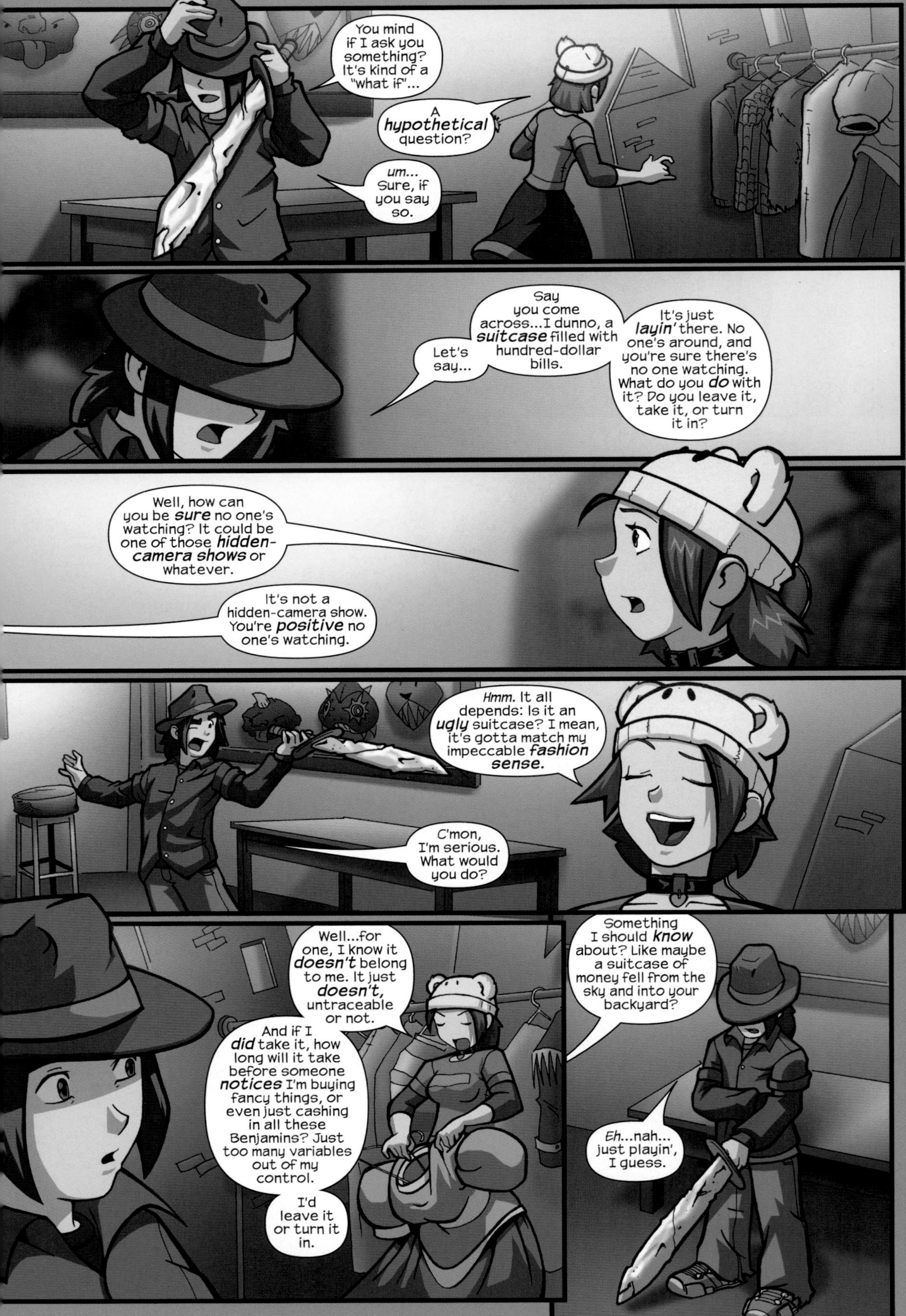
You mind if I ask you something? It's kind of a "what if"...
A hypothetical question?
um... Sure, if you say so.
Let's say...
Say you come across...I dunno, a suitcase filled with hundred-dollar bills.
It's just layin' there. No one's around, and you're sure there's no one watching. What do you do with it? Do you leave it, take it, or turn it in?
Well, how can you be sure no one's watching? It could be one of those hidden-camera shows or whatever.
It's not a hidden-camera show. You're positive no one's watching.
Hmm. It all depends: Is it an ugly suitcase? I mean, it's gotta match my impeccable fashion sense.
C'mon, I'm serious. What would you do?
Well...for one, I know it doesn't belong to me. It just doesn't, untraceable or not.
And if I did take it, how long will it take before someone notices I'm buying fancy things, or even just cashing in all these Benjamins? Just too many variables out of my control.
I'd leave it or turn it in.
Something I should know about? Like maybe a suitcase of money fell from the sky and into your backyard?
Eh...nah... just playin', I guess.

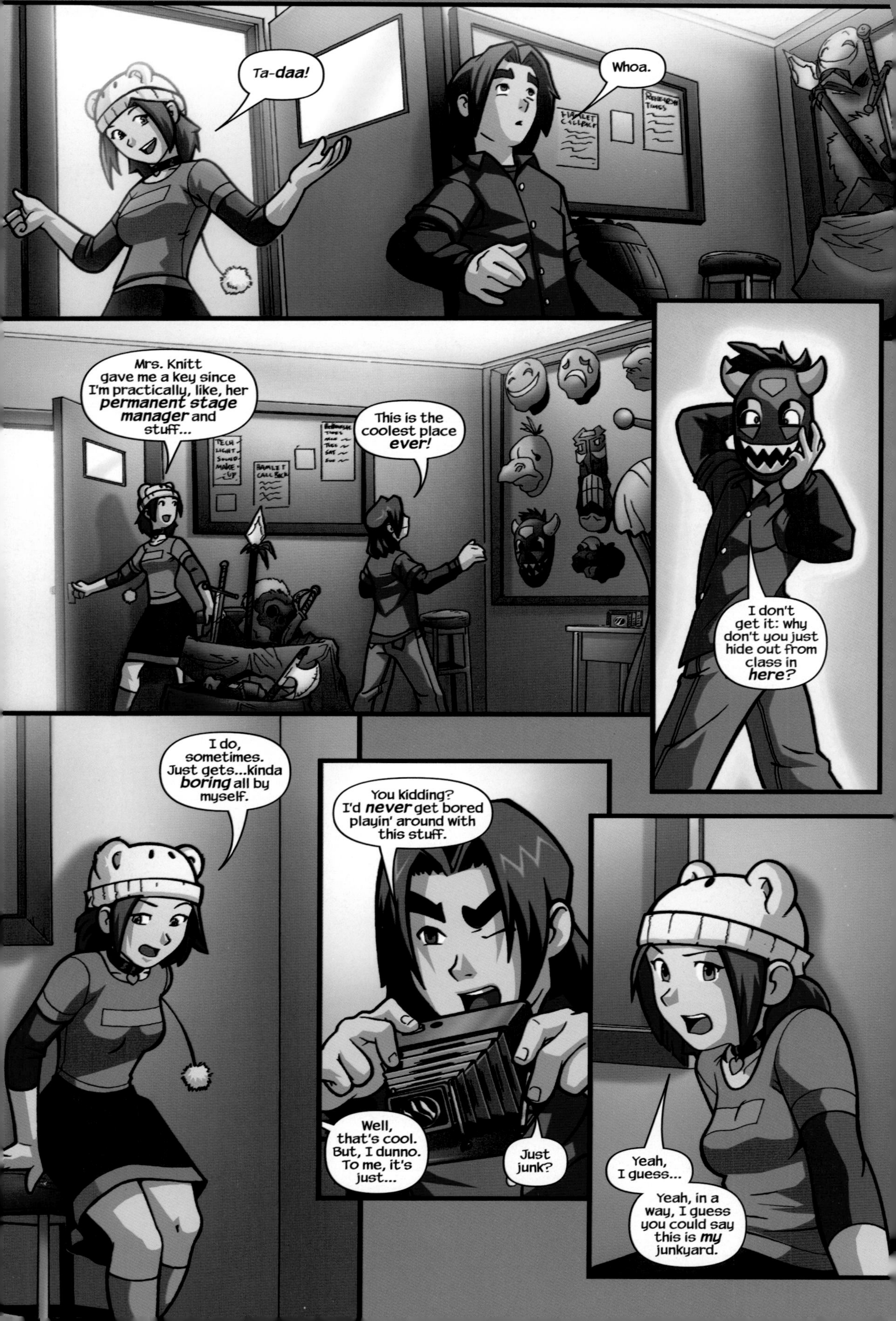
Ta-daa!
Whoa.
Mrs. Knitt gave me a key since I'm practically, like, her permanent stage manager and stuff...
This is the coolest place ever!
I don't get it: why don't you just hide out from class in here?
I do, sometimes. Just gets...kinda boring all by myself.
You kidding? I'd never get bored playin' around with this stuff.
Well, that's cool. But, I dunno. To me, it's just...
Just junk?
Yeah, I guess...
Yeah, in a way, I guess you could say this is my junkyard.

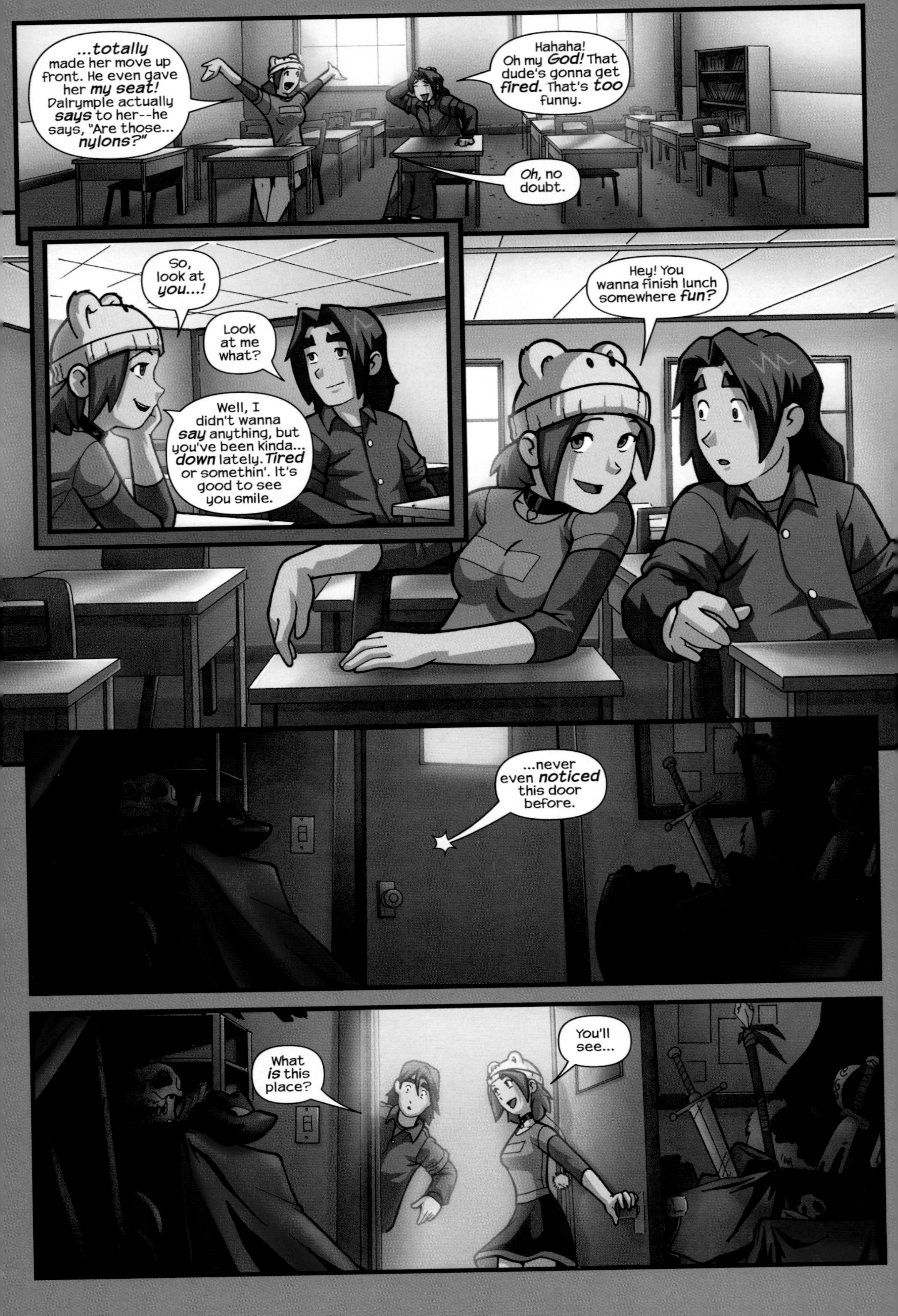
...totally made her move up front. He even gave her my seat! Dalrymple actually says to her--he says, "Are those... nylons?"
Hahaha! Oh my God! That dude's gonna get fired. That's too funny.
Oh, no doubt.
So, look at you...!
Look at me what?
Well, I didn't wanna say anything, but you've been kinda... down lately. Tired or somethin'. It's good to see you smile.
Hey! You wanna finish lunch somewhere fun?
...never even noticed this door before.
What is this place?
You'll see...

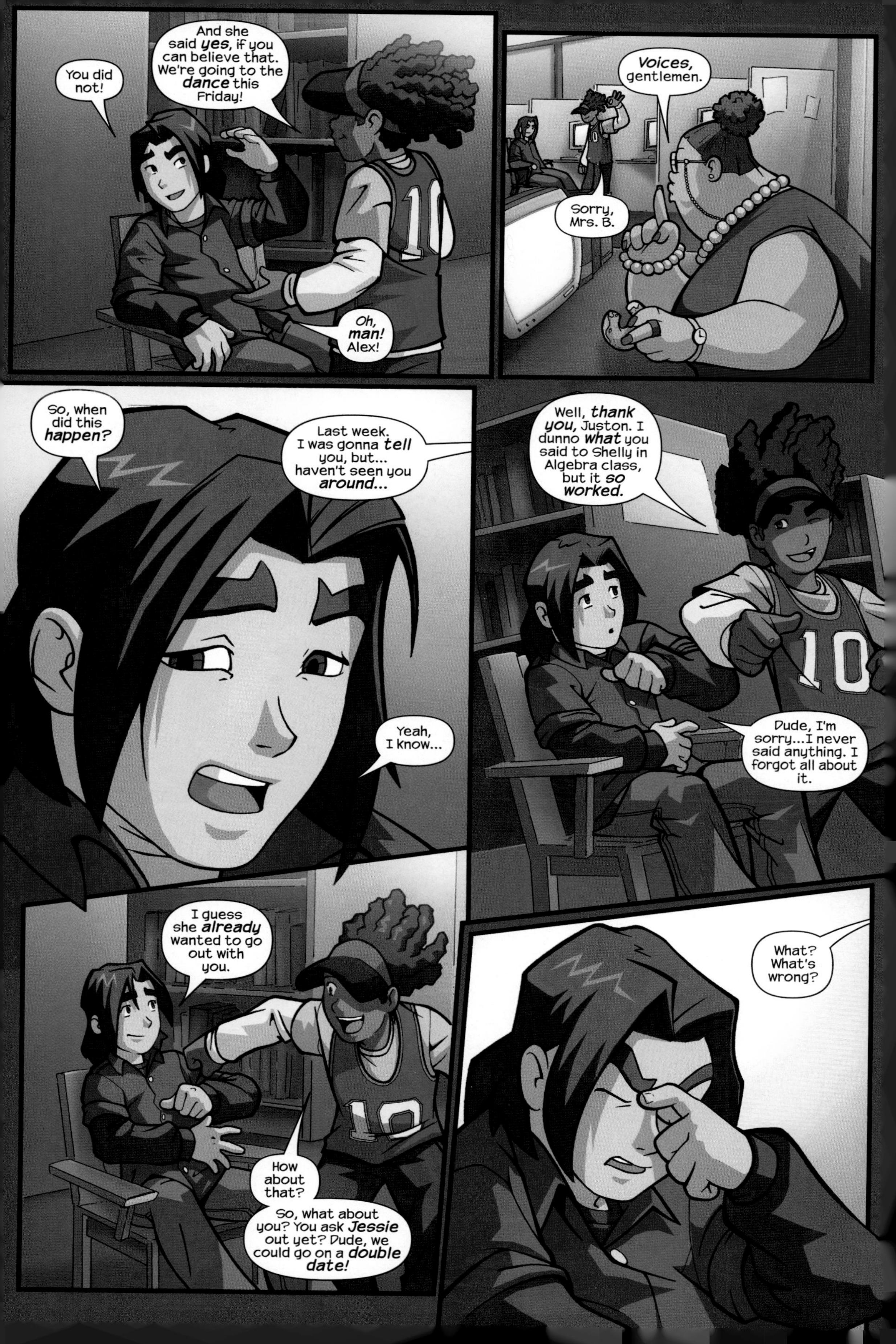
You did not!
And she said yes, if you can believe that. We're going to the dance this Friday!
Oh, man! Alex!
Voices, gentlemen.
Sorry, Mrs. B.
So, when did this happen?
Last week. I was gonna tell you, but... haven't seen you around...
Yeah, I know...
Well, thank you, Juston. I dunno what you said to Shelly in Algebra class, but it so worked.
Dude, I'm sorry...I never said anything. I forgot all about it.
I guess she already wanted to go out with you.
How about that?
So, what about you? You ask Jessie out yet? Dude, we could go on a double date!
What? What's wrong?

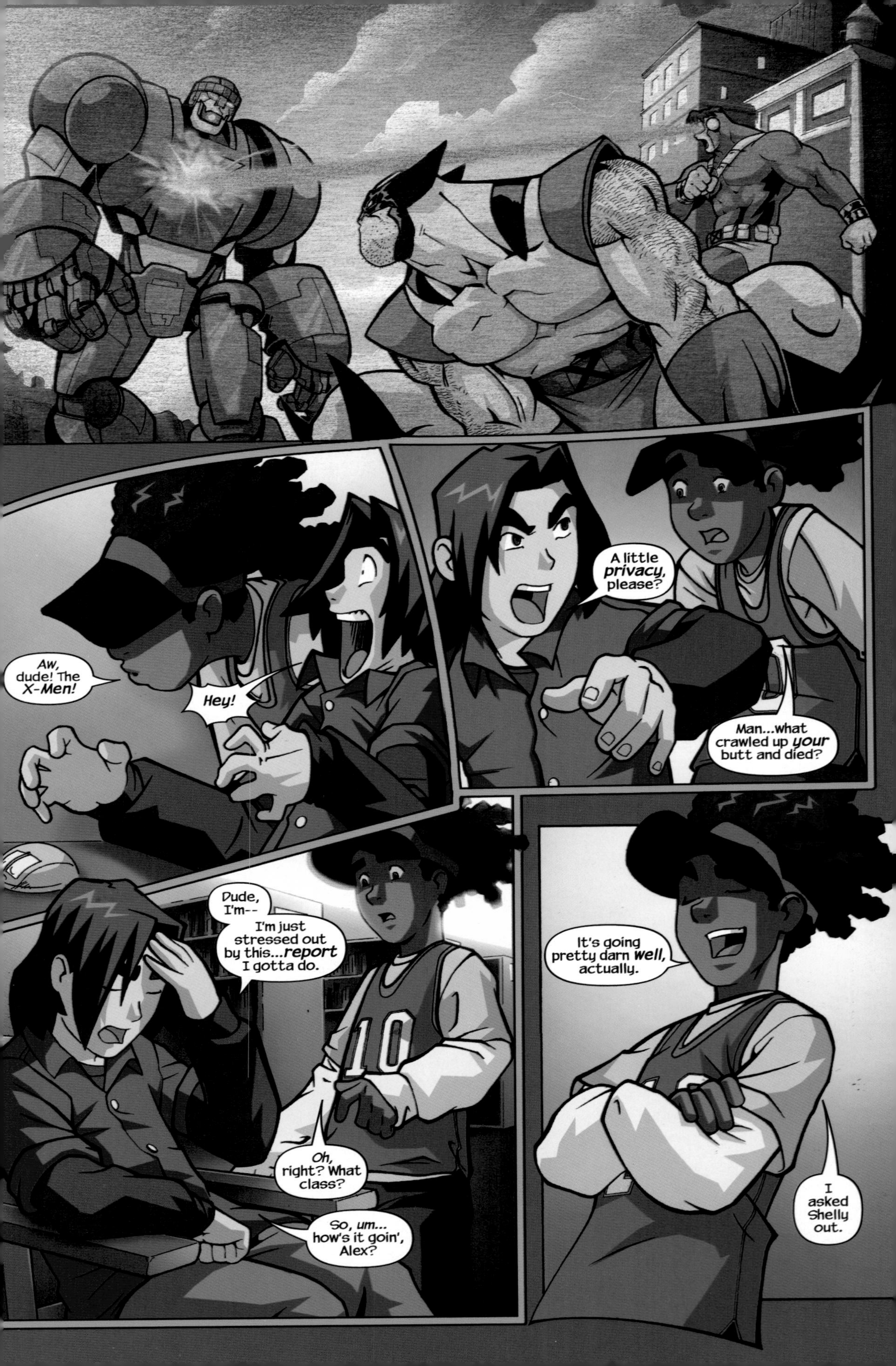
Aw, dude! The X-Men!
Hey!
A little privacy, please?
Man...what crawled up your butt and died?
Dude, I'm--
I'm just stressed out by this...report I gotta do.
Oh, right? What class?
So, um... how's it goin', Alex?
It's going pretty darn well, actually.
I asked Shelly out.

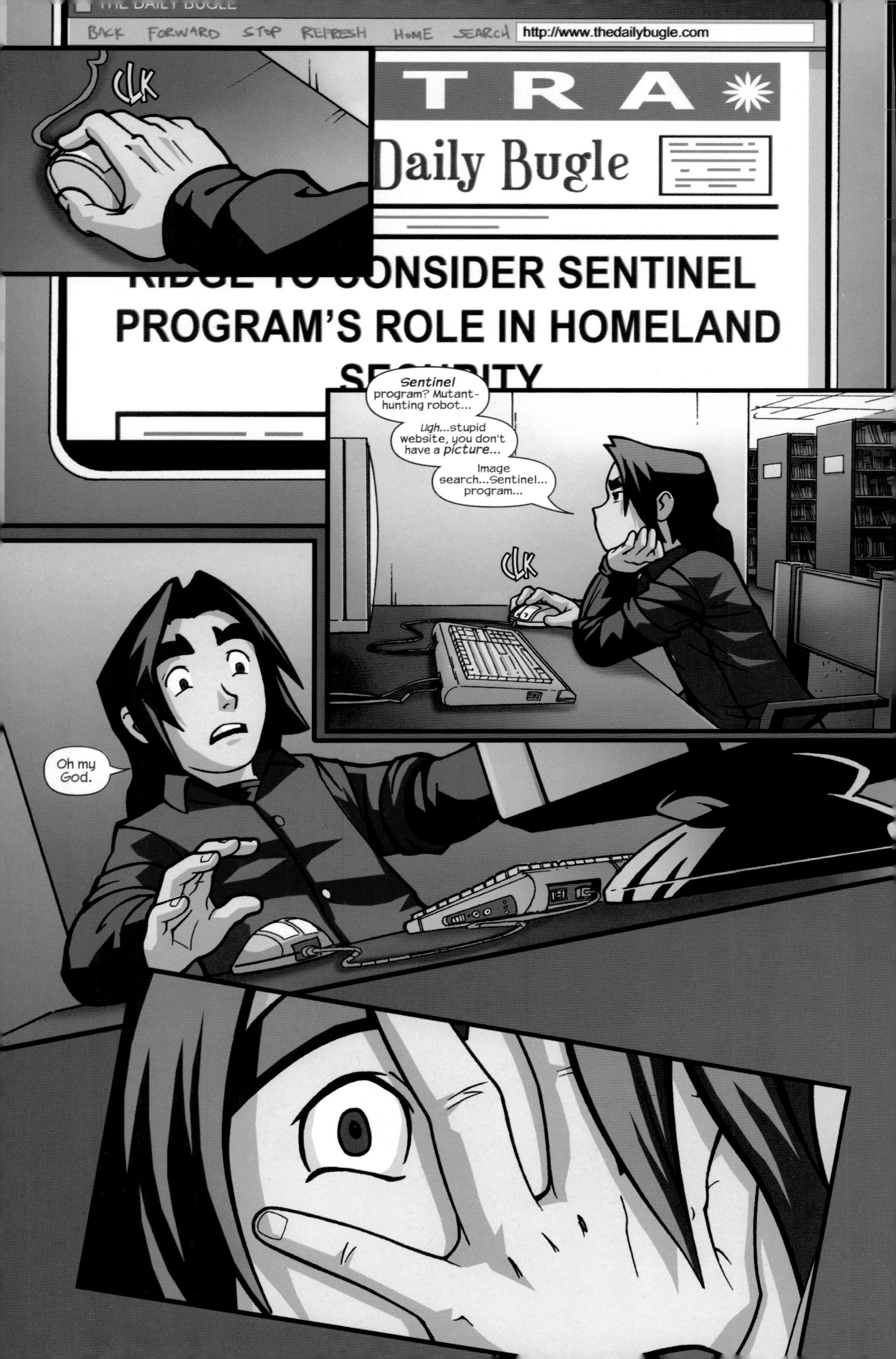
THE DAILY BUGLE
BACK FORWARD STOP REFRESH HOME SEARCH http://www.thedailybugle.com
CLK
TRA
Daily Bugle
CONSIDER SENTINEL
PROGRAM'S ROLE IN HOMELAND
Sentinel program? Mutant-hunting robot...
Ugh...stupid website, you don't have a picture...
Image search...Sentinel... program...
CLK
Oh my God.

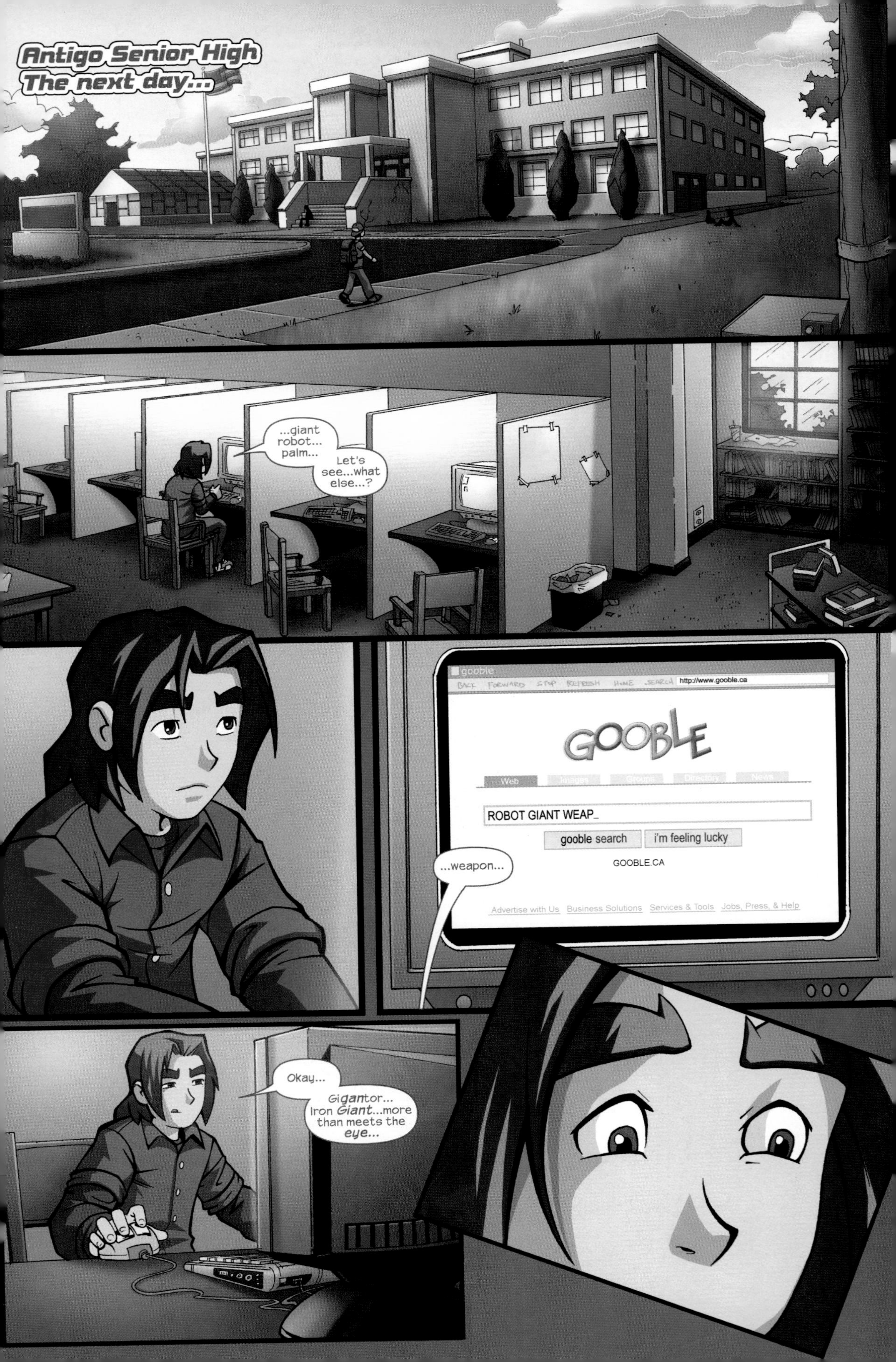
Antigo Senior High
The next day...
...giant robot... palm...
Let's see...what else...?
gooble
BACK FORWARD STOP REFRESH HOME SEARCH http://www.gooble.ca
GOOBLE
Web Images Groups Directory News
ROBOT GIANT WEAP_
gooble search
i'm feeling lucky
GOOBLE.CA
Advertise with Us Business Solutions Services & Tools Jobs, Press, & Help
...weapon...
Okay...
Gigantor... Iron Giant...more than meets the eye...

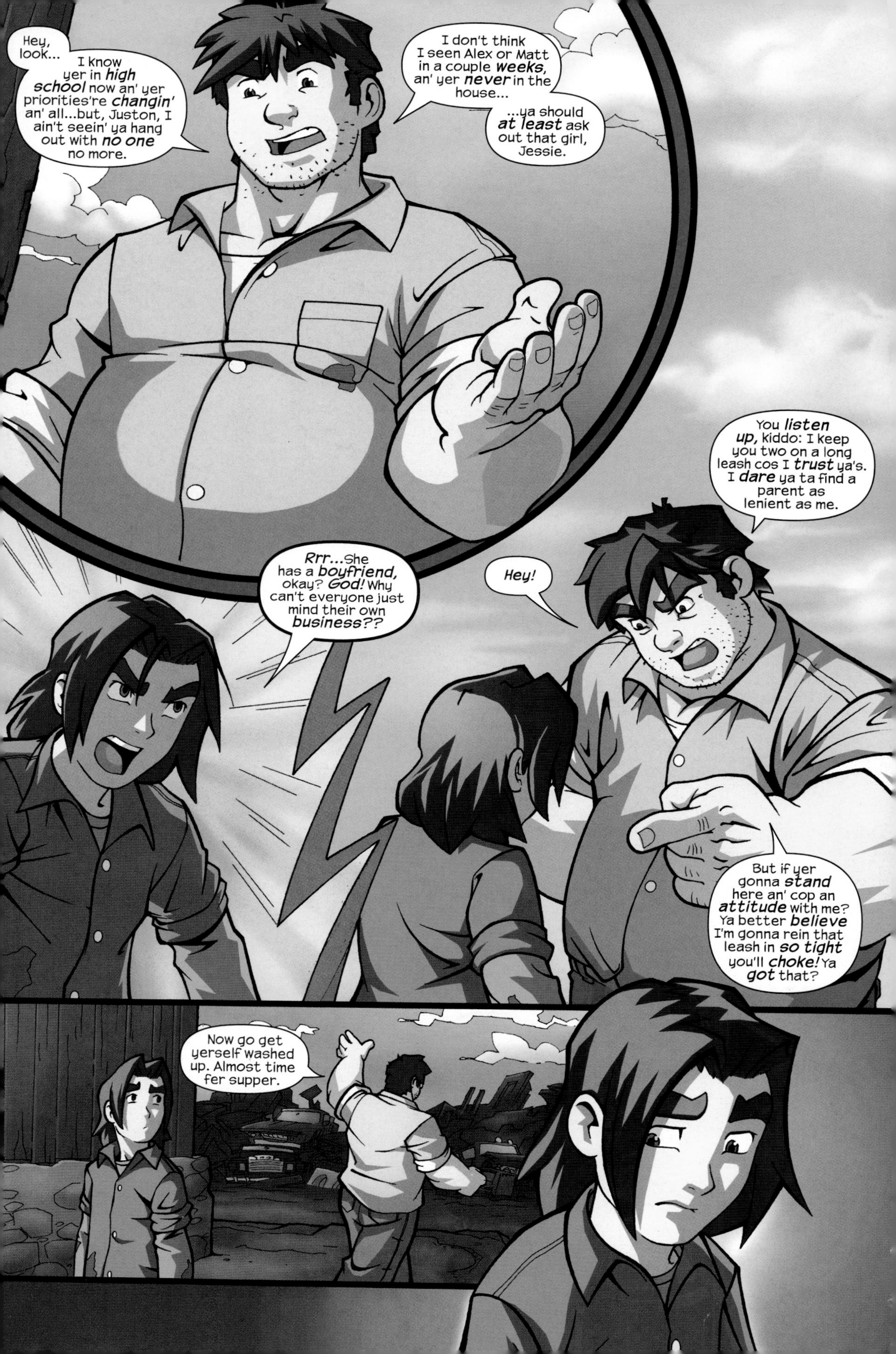
Hey, look...
I know yer in high school now an' yer priorities're changin' an' all...but, Juston, I ain't seein' ya hang out with no one no more.
I don't think I seen Alex or Matt in a couple weeks, an' yer never in the house...
...ya should at least ask out that girl, Jessie.
Rrr...She has a boyfriend, okay? God! Why can't everyone just mind their own business??
Hey!
You listen up, kiddo: I keep you two on a long leash cos I trust ya's. I dare ya ta find a parent as lenient as me.
But if yer gonna stand here an' cop an attitude with me? Ya better believe I'm gonna rein that leash in so tight you'll choke! Ya got that?
Now go get yerself washed up. Almost time fer supper.

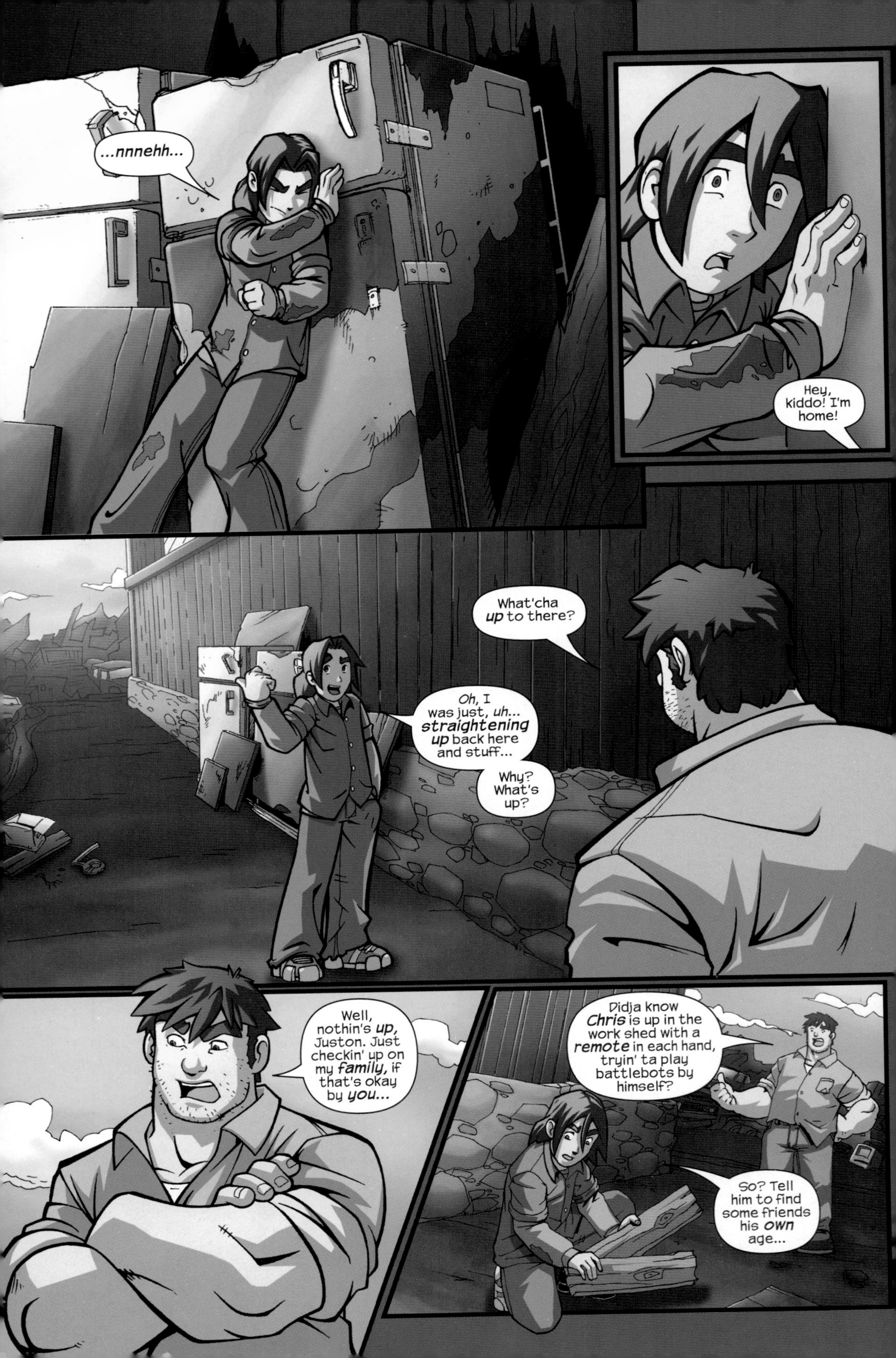
...nnnehh...
Hey, kiddo! I'm home!
What'cha *up* to there?
Oh, I was just, *uh*... ***straightening up*** back here and stuff...
Why? What's up?
Well, nothin's *up*, Juston. Just checkin' up on my *family*, if that's okay by *you*...
Didja know *Chris* is up in the work shed with a *remote* in each hand, tryin' ta play battlebots by himself?
So? Tell him to find some friends his *own* age...

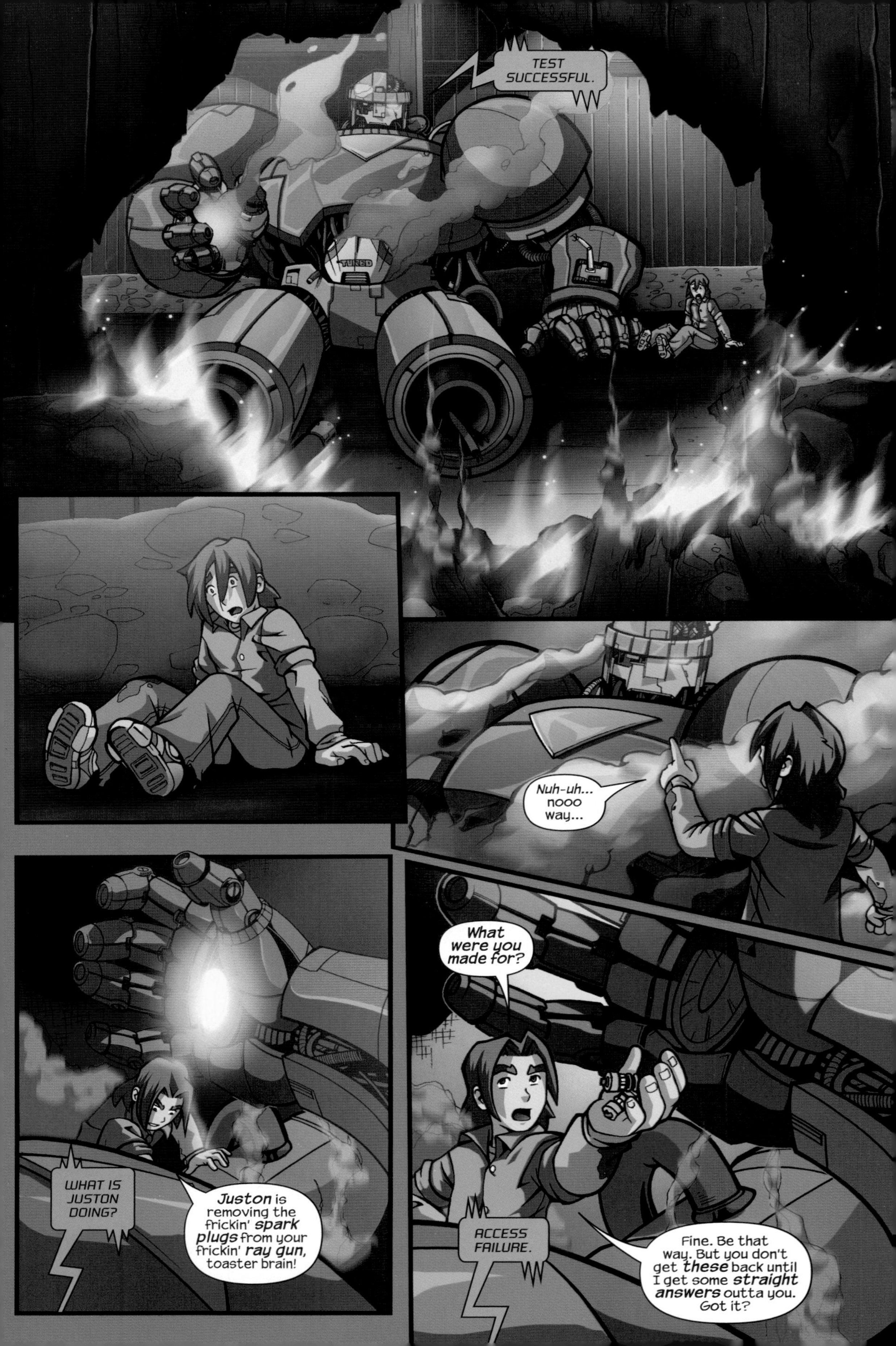
TEST SUCCESSFUL.
Nuh-uh... nooo way...
WHAT IS JUSTON DOING?
Juston is removing the frickin' spark plugs from your frickin' ray gun, toaster brain!
What were you made for?
ACCESS FAILURE.
Fine. Be that way. But you don't get these back until I get some straight answers outta you. Got it?

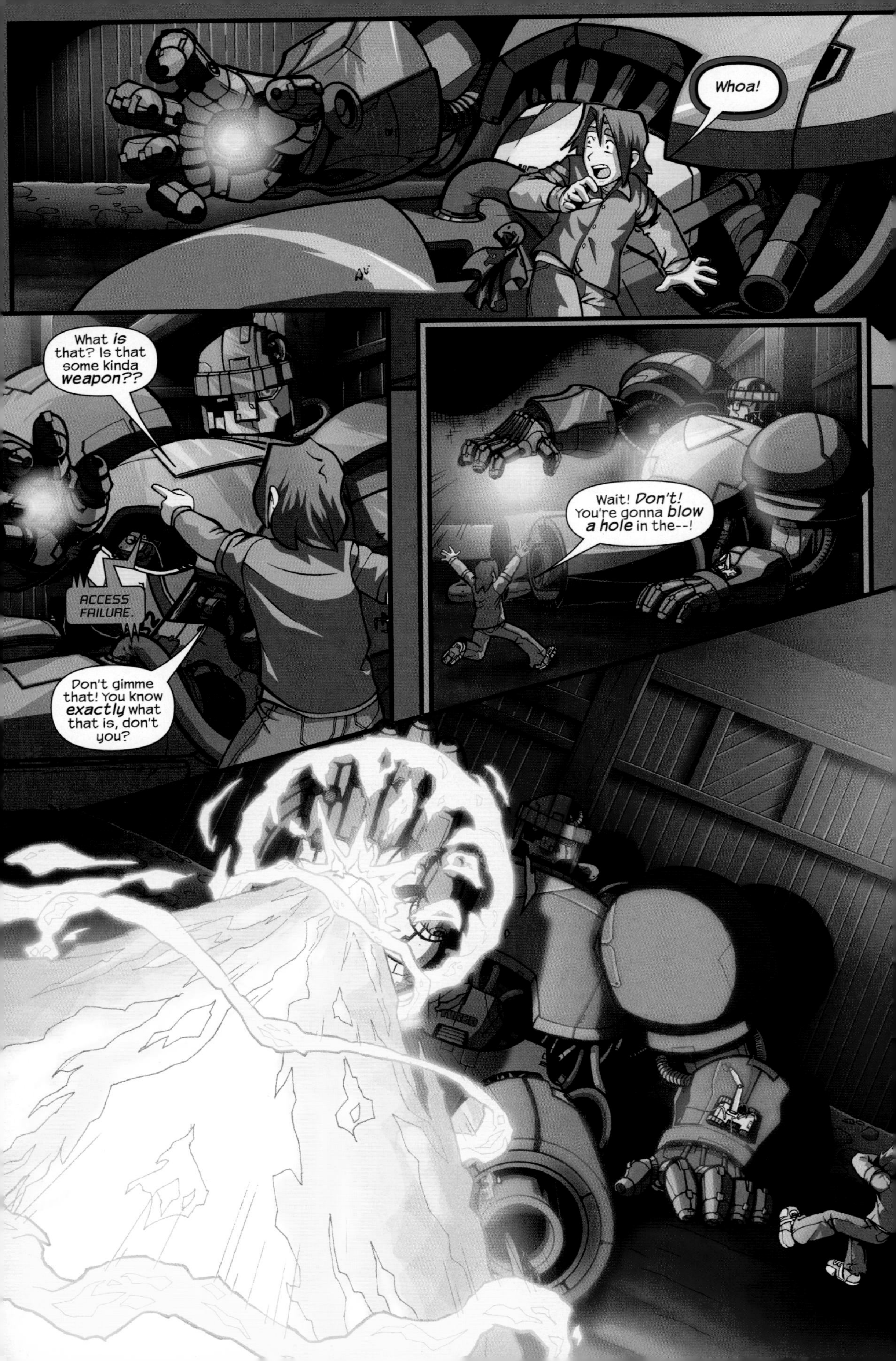
Whoa!
What is that? Is that some kinda weapon??
ACCESS FAILURE.
Don't gimme that! You know exactly what that is, don't you?
Wait! Don't! You're gonna blow a hole in the--!
TURBO

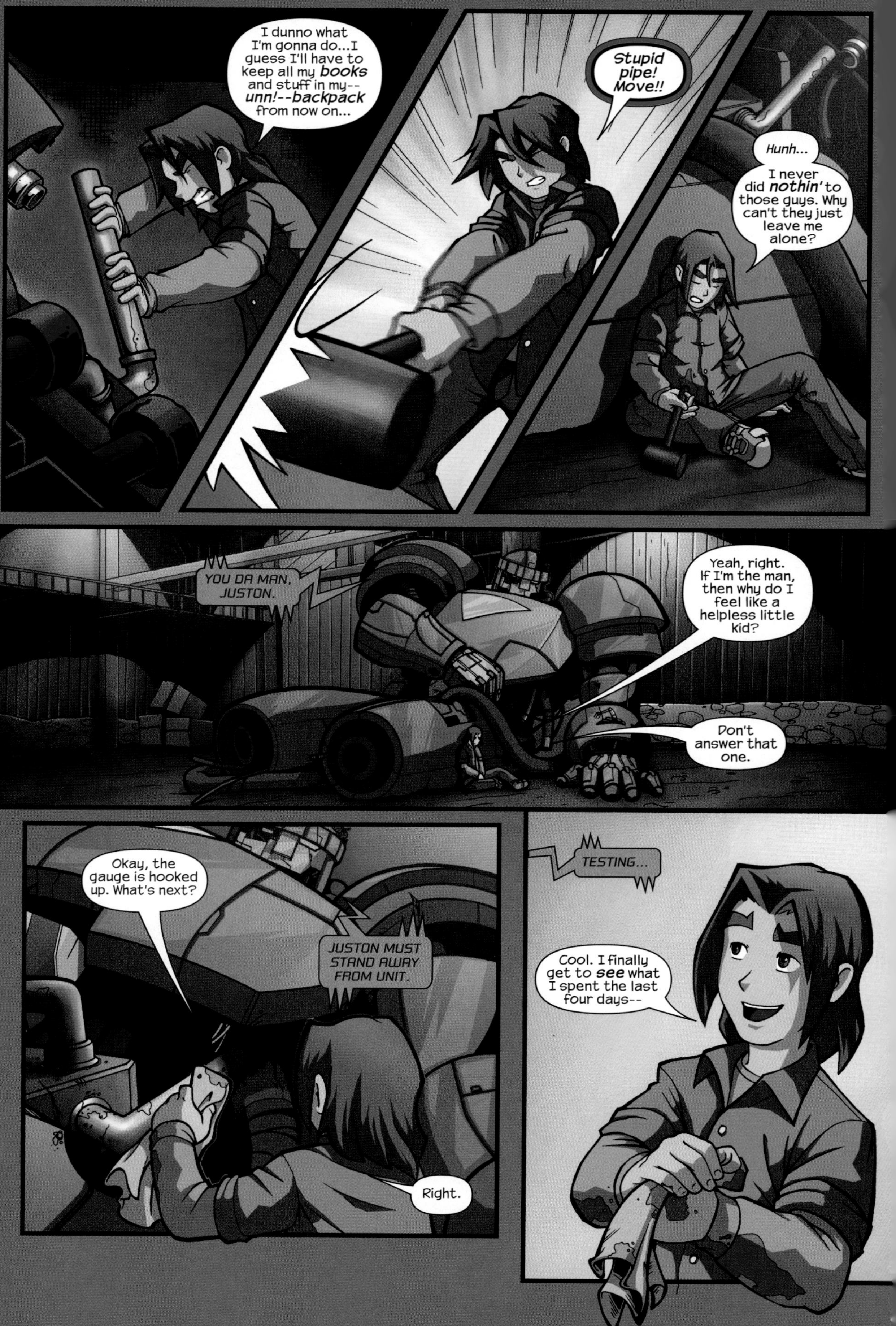
I dunno what I'm gonna do...I guess I'll have to keep all my books and stuff in my-- unn!--backpack from now on...
Stupid pipe! Move!!
Hunh...
I never did nothin' to those guys. Why can't they just leave me alone?
YOU DA MAN, JUSTON.
Yeah, right. If I'm the man, then why do I feel like a helpless little kid?
Don't answer that one.
Okay, the gauge is hooked up. What's next?
JUSTON MUST STAND AWAY FROM UNIT.
Right.
TESTING...
Cool. I finally get to see what I spent the last four days--

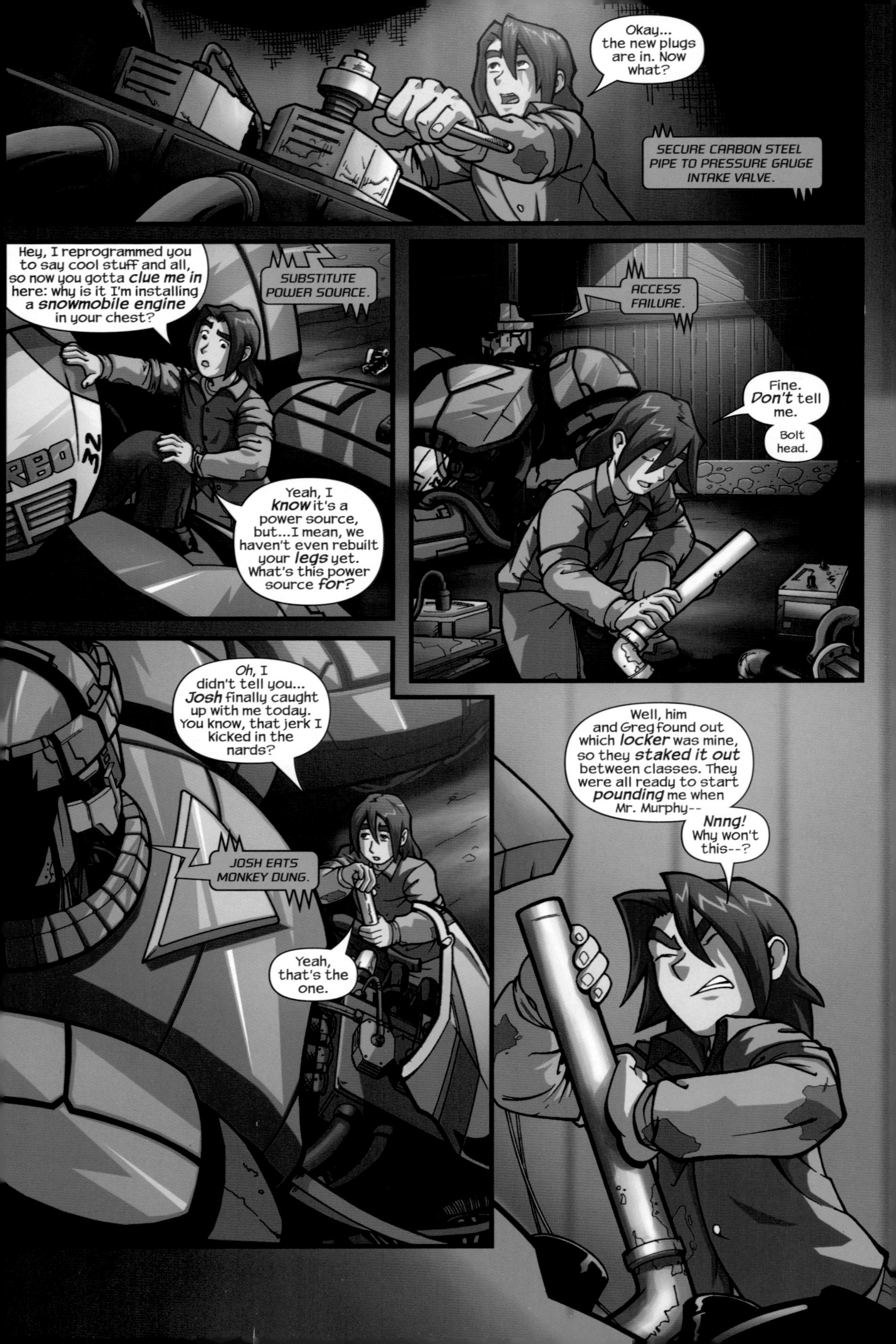

Okay... the new plugs are in. Now what?
SECURE CARBON STEEL PIPE TO PRESSURE GAUGE INTAKE VALVE.
Hey, I reprogrammed you to say cool stuff and all, so now you gotta clue me in here: why is it I'm installing a snowmobile engine in your chest?
SUBSTITUTE POWER SOURCE.
Yeah, I know it's a power source, but...I mean, we haven't even rebuilt your legs yet. What's this power source for?
ACCESS FAILURE.
Fine. Don't tell me.
Bolt head.
Oh, I didn't tell you... Josh finally caught up with me today. You know, that jerk I kicked in the nards?
JOSH EATS MONKEY DUNG.
Yeah, that's the one.
Well, him and Greg found out which locker was mine, so they staked it out between classes. They were all ready to start pounding me when Mr. Murphy--
Nnng! Why won't this--?

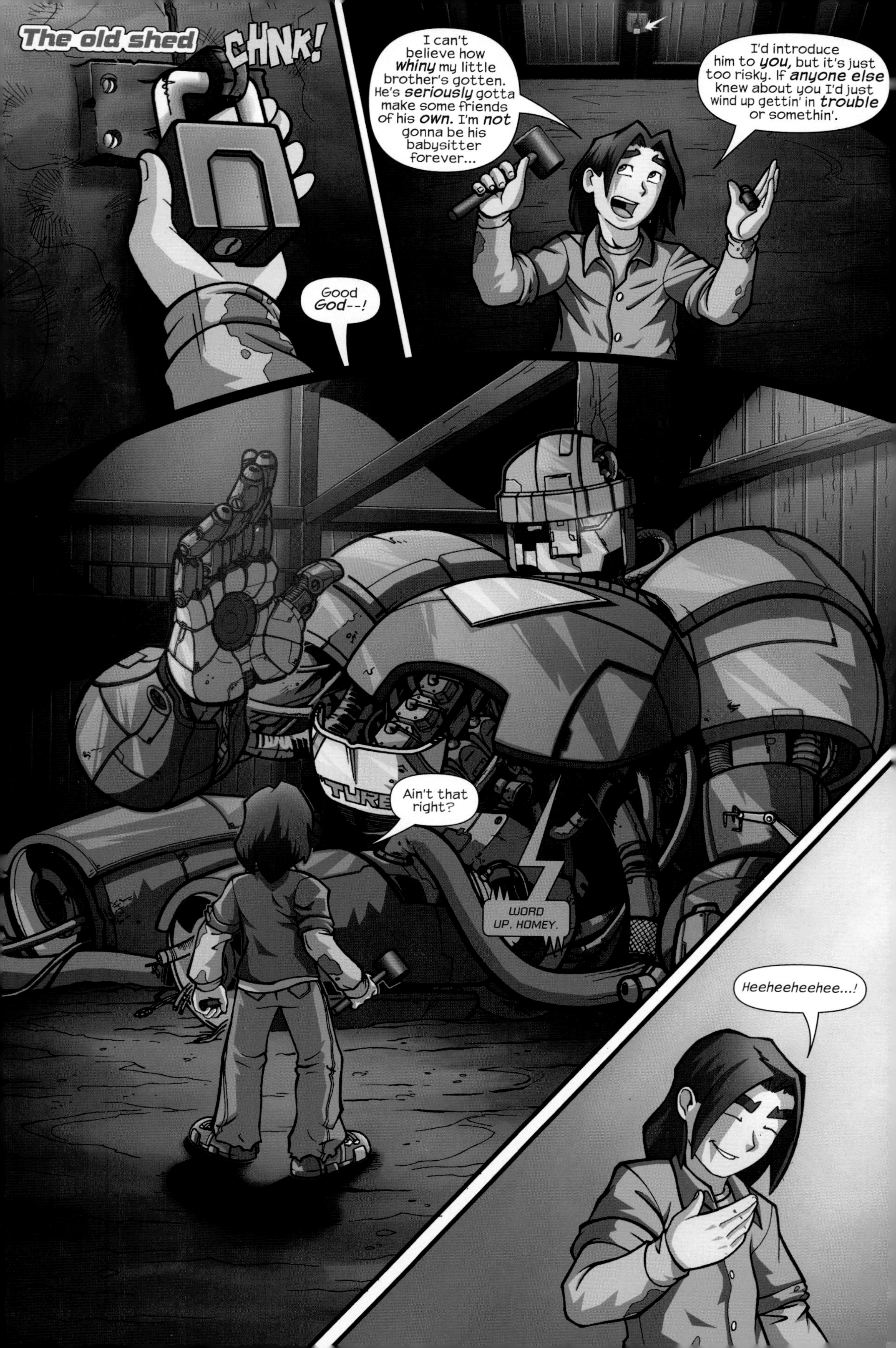
The old shed
CHNK!
Good God--!
I can't believe how whiny my little brother's gotten. He's seriously gotta make some friends of his own. I'm not gonna be his babysitter forever...
I'd introduce him to you, but it's just too risky. If anyone else knew about you I'd just wind up gettin' in trouble or somethin'.
Ain't that right?
WORD UP, HOMEY.
Heeheeheehee...!

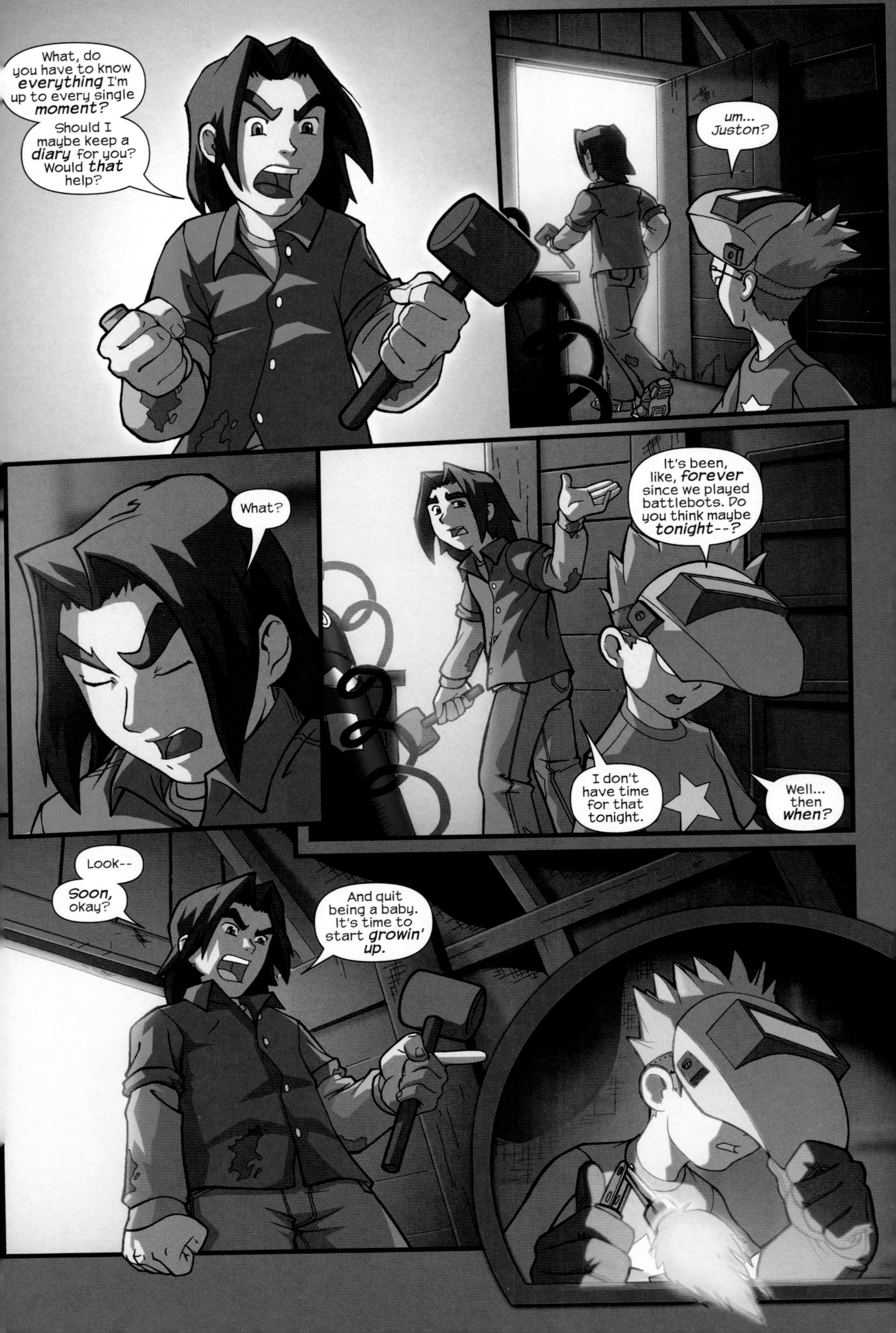

What, do you have to know everything I'm up to every single moment? Should I maybe keep a diary for you? Would that help?
um... Juston?
What?
It's been, like, forever since we played battlebots. Do you think maybe tonight--?
I don't have time for that tonight.
Well... then when?
Look--
Soon, okay?
And quit being a baby. It's time to start growin' up.

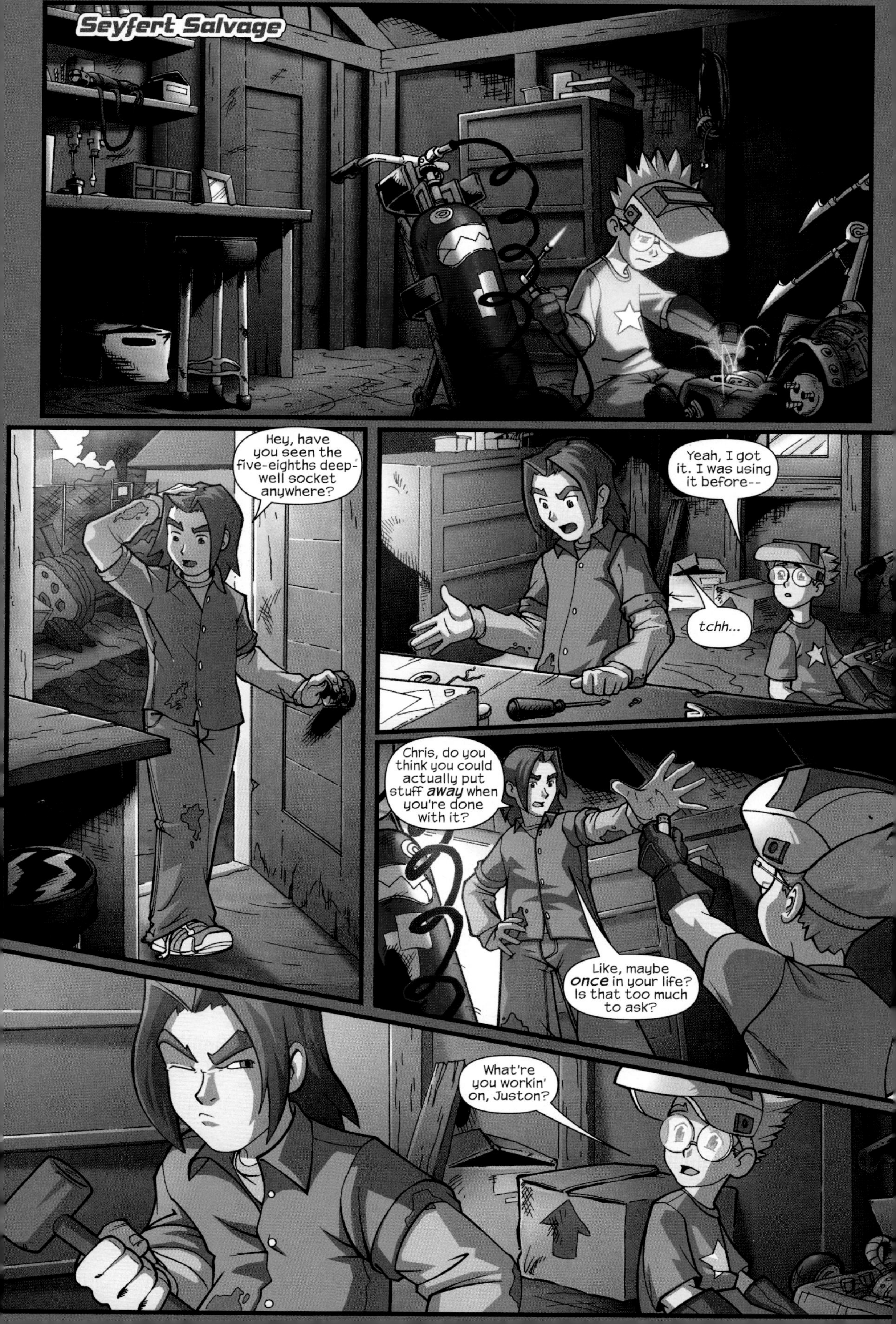
Seyfert Salvage
Hey, have you seen the five-eighths deep-well socket anywhere?
Yeah, I got it. I was using it before--
tchh...
Chris, do you think you could actually put stuff *away* when you're done with it?
Like, maybe *once* in your life? Is that too much to ask?
What're you workin' on, Juston?

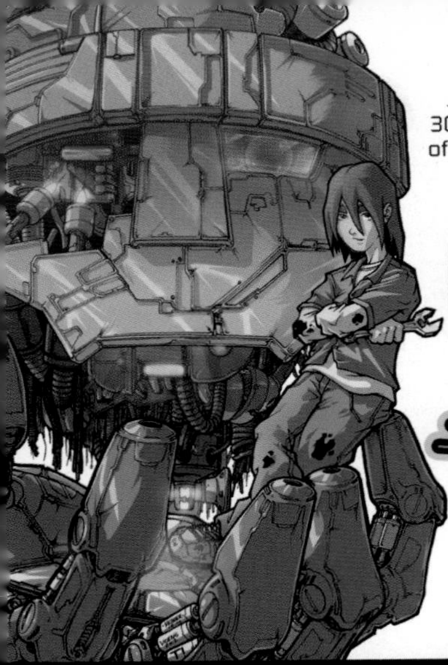

Juston Seyfert has just made the discovery of a lifetime: the damaged remains of a 30-foot-tall robot, buried in his father's junkyard! But will his discovery lead to the birth of a new hero...or to unbridled revenge for a life full of hardships...? Stan Lee Presents:

SENTINEL

"SALVAGE"
part 3

Previously...

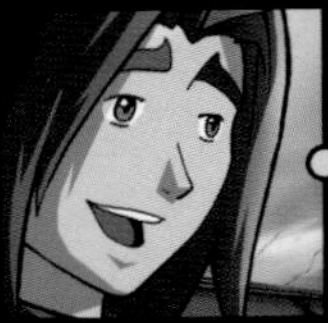

Juston Seyfert
Our Hero

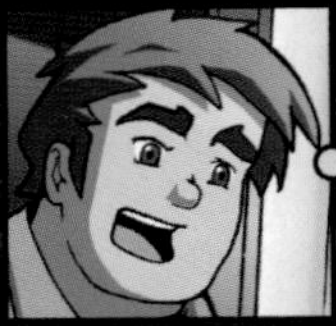

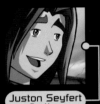

Pete Seyfert
His Dad

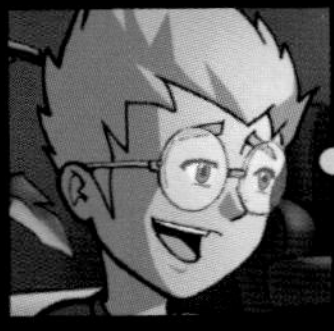

Chris Seyfert
Little Bro

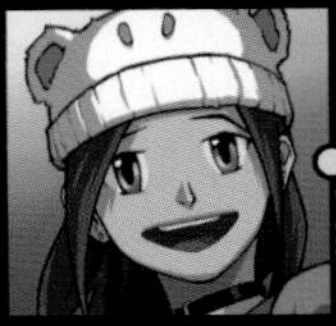

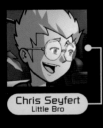

Jessie
The Dream Girl

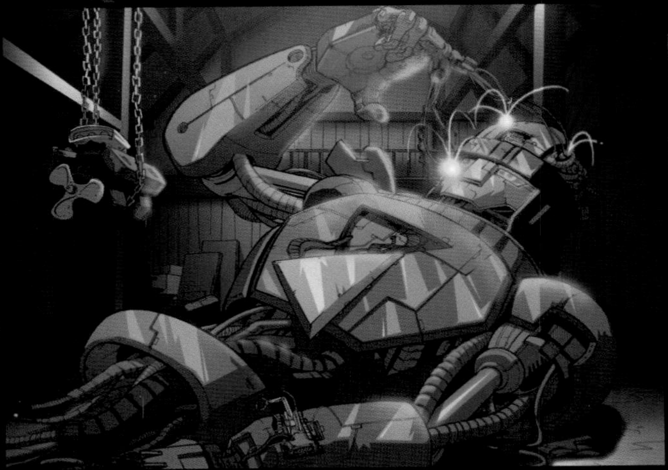

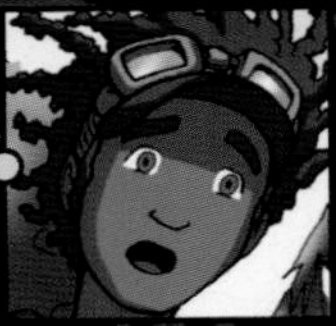

Alex
Best Friend, Part 1

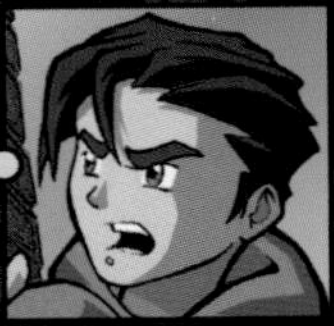

Matt
Best Friend, the Sequel

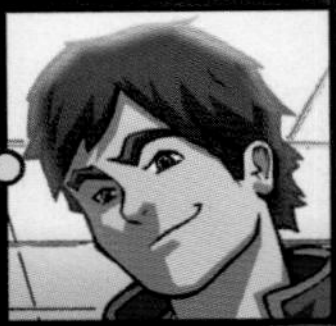

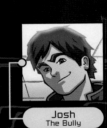

Josh
The Bully

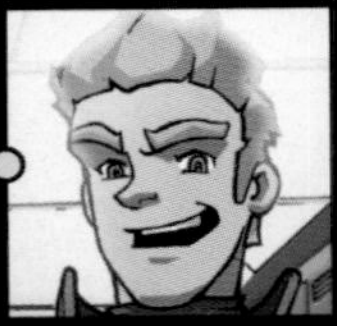

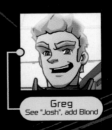

Greg
See "Josh", add Blond

You might think that it sucks to be Juston Seyfert. He's tormented by the Seniors at Antigo High School. He has no luck with the ladies. He's dirt poor. He lives in his father's junkyard. And his mother walked out on him and his family years ago. Yeah, you might think that it sucks...but, oddly enough,you'd be wrong.

Through a chance lunch-time encounter, Juston has met the girl of his dreams: a Senior named Jessie. Not only is she fun, smart and absolutely gorgeous, but she's taken a liking to Juston and actually seems to appreciate him for who he is...which, to Juston, is a rarity!

Just when things didn't look like they could get much better, Juston made a discovery that turned his world even more upside-down: a gigantic, half-broken robot that had somehow found its way into the shed at the back of his family's junkyard! Once the initial rush of terror died down, Juston couldn't have been more thrilled!

Although the robot's origins remain unknown, Juston has decided to keep his find a secret from the world--including his family and friends. Using his strong technical skills--developed from years of playing in the scrap--Juston has made the rebuilding and reprogramming of this technological wonder his "pet project."

But the question remains: once the job is done, what the heck is Juston going to do with this 30-foot-tall mechanical monstrosity?!?

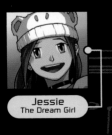

VISIT US AT
www.abdopublishing.com

Reinforced library bound edition published in 2007 by Spotlight, a division of the ABDO Publishing Group, Edina, Minnesota. Spotlight produces high-quality reinforced library bound editions for schools and libraries. Published by agreement with Marvel Characters, Inc.

Library of Congress Cataloging-in-Publication Data

McKeever, Sean.
Sentinel / [story, Sean McKeever ; pencils and inks, UDON ... et al.].
v. cm.
Cover title.
Revisions of issues 1-6 of the serial Sentinel.
"Marvel Age."
Contents: #1. Salvage -- #2. Discovery -- #3. Pet project -- #4. Rebuilding -- #5. Test mission -- #6. Primary targets.
ISBN-13: 978-1-59961-316-1 (v. 1)
ISBN-10: 1-59961-316-6 (v. 1)
ISBN-13: 978-1-59961-317-8 (v. 2)
ISBN-10: 1-59961-317-4 (v. 2)
ISBN-13: 978-1-59961-318-5 (v. 3)
ISBN-10: 1-59961-318-2 (v. 3)
ISBN-13: 978-1-59961-319-2 (v. 4)
ISBN-10: 1-59961-319-0 (v. 4)
ISBN-13: 978-1-59961-320-8 (v. 5)
ISBN-10: 1-59961-320-4 (v. 5)
ISBN-13: 978-1-59961-321-5 (v. 6)
ISBN-10: 1-59961-321-2 (v. 6)
1. Comic books, strips, etc. I. UDON. II. Title. III. Title: Salvage. IV. Title: Discovery. V. Title: Pet project. VI. Title: Rebuilding. VII. Title: Test mission. VIII. Title: Primary targets.

PN6728.S453 M35 2007
741.5'973--dc22

2006050623

Spotlight

All Spotlight books are reinforced library binding
and manufactured in the United States of America.

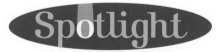

SENTINEL

Story: Sean McKeever

Art by UDON

Pencils and Inks: Vriens, Heilig, Hepburn, and Vedder

Colors: Hou, Yan, and Yeung   UDON Chief: Erik Ko   Letters: Cory Petit

Assistant Editor: Andy Schmidt   Editor: Marc Sumerak   Editor in Chief: Joe Quesada

President: Bill Jemas

PET PROJECT

PART 3

MARVEL   Spotlight